LAURENCE YEP
PICTURES BY KAM MAK

The Dragon Prince

A CHINESE BEAUTY & THE BEAST TALE

HARPERCOLLINSPUBLISHERS

Acknowledgments

The Dragon Prince is a Southern Chinese version of a traditional Chinese tale.
My thanks to Truly Shay for her help in translating several tales for me.
—Laurence Yep

Thanks to Sinotique for allowing me to photograph some of its antiques.
—Kam Mak

Library of Congress Cataloging-in-Publication Data
Yep, Laurence.
The Dragon prince: a Chinese Beauty & the beast tale / Laurence Yep ; pictures by Kam Mak.
p.   cm.
Summary: A poor farmer's youngest daughter agrees to marry a fierce dragon in order
to save her father's life.
ISBN 0-06-024381-3. — ISBN 0-06-443518-0 (pbk.)
[1. Fairy tales.   2. Folklore—China.]   I. Mak, Kim, ill.   II. Title.
PZ8.Y46Dr   1997   95-11091
[398.2'0951'02—dc20   CIP
AC

Typography by Al Cetta. Title lettering by Leah Preiss.
17 SCP 25 24 23 22
❖
Visit us on the World Wide Web!
http://www.harperchildrens.com

To Joanne

—L.Y.

For my wife, Mari, and for my daughter, Luca

—K.M.

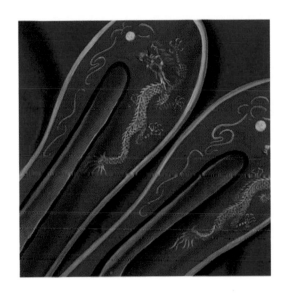

Once there was a poor old farmer with seven daughters. The land was so barren that he grew more rocks than rice. The family would have starved if it had not been for the youngest and prettiest daughter, Seven. She could weave the finest silk and embroider the fanciest stitchery. Under her needle, unicorns, dragons, and other magical beasts came to life. Her work was famous among the noble families of the province.

The third daughter, Three, was jealous of Seven. "How come Seven gets to stay home while I have to work in the dirt?" she asked.

The farmer scolded her: "Because she cooks and cleans and does the work of three while you spend all the day plucking one weed!"

One afternoon, when their father had gone to town to sell Seven's silk, Three found a golden serpent in the rice fields and raised her hoe to kill it.

Seven had brought her family's dinner down to the fields. "No, it's just a little water serpent." Stopping her sister, the kind girl picked up the serpent and left it outside their fields. "Shame on you for scaring my sister," Seven said, setting the serpent down and walking away.

he serpent wriggled right to the hills to a cave, where he began to dance in circles until he changed into a huge dragon.

That afternoon, as the farmer returned home, the dragon sprang from the nearby cave and seized the farmer in its paw. "Give me one of your daughters for a wife, and I'll give you your life as her bride price."

"I couldn't order any of them to do a terrible thing like that," the farmer cried.

"Then prepare to die." And the dragon raised a paw with claws as sharp as daggers.

"No, wait," the old farmer cried out in fright.

Just then, the oldest daughter came looking for him. When she saw the dragon clutching her father, she shrieked, "Papa, come home. Seven has made rice and fresh fish soup especially for your supper."

"My darling oldest child," the farmer said, "if you don't marry this dragon, I'll be *his* supper."

"I'm sorry, Papa, but your supper will just have to get cold," she answered, and ran away to hide.

o it went with the next five daughters, until Seven herself came to find the rest of her family. When she saw the giant golden dragon, she walked slowly toward it, saying, "Papa, come home. I've made rice and fresh fish soup especially for your supper."

The old farmer tried one last time. "My sweetest child, if you don't marry this dragon, I'll be *his* supper."

Seven's eyes measured the sharpness of the dragon's teeth and claws and the power of its armored body, and she was afraid. Yet she could not let her father suffer such a terrible fate. "Then you can have your supper, Papa, because I will marry the dragon."

Releasing the farmer, the dragon reared up into the air. "Climb onto my back."

As soon as Seven did, the dragon shot into the night sky like a meteor.

Higher and higher they soared over hills and mountains, past deserts and seas, on and on, until the sleeping world became a ball of dark velvet and the lakes silvery sequins. Still higher and farther the dragon raced, until the Milky Way wound its way across the night sky like an endless bolt of the whitest silk.

They flew so fast that they caught up with the moon, which shone like a giant pearl upon the sea. And within the sea lay towns and strange gardens and waving forests of kelp.

With one last surge, they plunged beneath the surface to a vast palace of living coral. Seven found she could breathe beneath the water. Setting her on her feet in the courtyard, the dragon kept his paw around her. "Aren't you frightened? I could crush you like a twig."

For a moment, Seven stood utterly still in his paws, gazing up at the dragon's face. His scales gleamed like jewels in a golden net, and his eyes shone like twin suns. It was a face of terror and a face of beauty. It was a face of magic.

Slowly, she stretched out her arm, and for a moment his large head flinched from her tiny hand.

"I know the loom and stove and many ordinary things," she said, "but my hand has never touched wonder."

This time, when she stretched out her hand, his head remained still, but the big eyes watched her.

Gently, she stroked his cheek. "You are beautiful."

"*You* are beautiful," the dragon replied. "But you really *should* be frightened," he insisted.

Seven smiled. "The eye sees what it will, but the heart sees what it should. If you had meant to harm me, you would have done so already."

"I've worn many disguises and scoured the sky, land, and sea, but I haven't found anyone who is your match. You are brave and kind and true as well as beautiful!" the dragon cried. He leaped away from her and began to dance, curling his powerful body as easily as a giant golden ribbon. And overhead, on the surface of the sea, the moon seemed to dissolve and fuse again like a school of fish darting this way and that.

Then he began to spin in the water until he became a column of light, and from the light stepped a handsome prince. "Now will it be such a terrible fate to marry me?" he asked.

Seven took his hand. "No," she laughed.

even now wore elegant silk robes, dined on the rarest delicacies from gold plates, and drank from jade cups. A dozen maids obeyed her slightest whim. Even so, she was not used to being idle and asked for a loom. But now she embroidered only golden dragons on shoes she made just for her prince.

But as the days passed, Seven became sad and lost her appetite. When her husband asked her the reason, she told him she missed her family.

Then he said, "I understand it is the custom among your kind that brides may visit their families after they marry, but you must come back in ten days."

even promised. That very night she slipped into her finest robe and put on her jewelry, while her maids decorated her hair with precious pearls and jade.

When she was ready, she climbed into a chair of gold and coral, and her servants lifted her out of the sea and into the air. Behind her chair flew all her maids. Her family was astounded the next morning when the glittering procession descended from the sky. Seven bowed to her father and greeted her sisters.

"**Y**ou'll never have to work or go hungry again with all the gifts I've brought you," she said. When Seven told them all about her husband, the family was happy for her—except for Three. Three envied her sister's jewels and clothes and servants. "They should have been mine," she said to herself.

So the next day she took Seven down to the river for a picnic. There she asked her, "Little sister, may I try on your things?"

To please Three, Seven exchanged clothes with her and let her put on her jewelry. Then they went down to the river to look at their reflections. But as Seven leaned over to see her image, Three knocked her on the head and shoved her into the river.

When Three told the rest of the family what she had done, she warned them, "The Prince will come back as a dragon and eat us all if you don't do what I say."

And they were so afraid that they did. They told Seven's servants that she had fallen ill and sent a message to the Prince. "Don't be surprised if she looks different," they told him. When the Prince heard, he didn't care. In that short time, Seven had come to mean everything to him, not for her beauty but for her kindness.

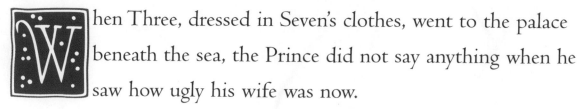hen Three, dressed in Seven's clothes, went to the palace beneath the sea, the Prince did not say anything when he saw how ugly his wife was now.

He was surprised, though, when she did not know where anything was—not even her room. She was all thumbs at the loom, and her embroidery stitches were ugly and clumsy. "It's the illness," Three lied. "It's made me forget everything. Why do you pick on me? You will make me sick again."

Though the Prince apologized, he was uncertain, for neither his eyes nor his heart saw what they should. "This cannot be my Seven," he thought. He told Three he was going to hunt, but he did not tell her for what. Determined to discover the truth, he set out for the world above.

even had not drowned. Down the river, an old woman had found her and taken her home. Seven was very sick, and the old woman nursed her for a long time.

When Seven finally woke and told the old woman who she was, the old woman smiled. "You're confused, dear. You can't be that lucky girl. She returned to her husband already."

To her dismay, Seven realized what had happened and shook her head. "My husband searched the world for someone who would be true, and yet he himself is not. He could not even tell the difference between me and my sister. And my family has betrayed me as well."

The old woman felt sorry for Seven. "Why don't you stay with me for a while, until you are well," she said.

So Seven stayed with the old woman and wove the silk and embroidered the shoes that the old woman sold in the marketplace.

eanwhile, the Prince searched everywhere for clues of his lost love. One day, he happened to pass through the market and saw the pair of shoes that the old woman was selling. Embroidered on the cloth were giant golden dragons dancing above the waves beneath the full moon.

Hardly daring to hope, his heart pounding, the Prince bought the shoes without bargaining and then followed the old woman back to her shack.

As soon as he saw Seven, he rushed inside. "I've been looking everywhere for you."

"I wasn't sure," Seven confessed. "I heard that my sister Three took my place."

He smiled. "But not in my heart, which saw what it should. So you will come home with me?"

"Yes," said Seven.

And the Prince transformed himself into his dragon shape, and with Seven and the old woman on his back, he flew to his palace beneath the sea.

They sent the shame-faced Three back to her family. And then Seven and the Prince and the old woman settled down to a long and happy life together.